[redacted]

Libby Wimbley

Bug Rescuer

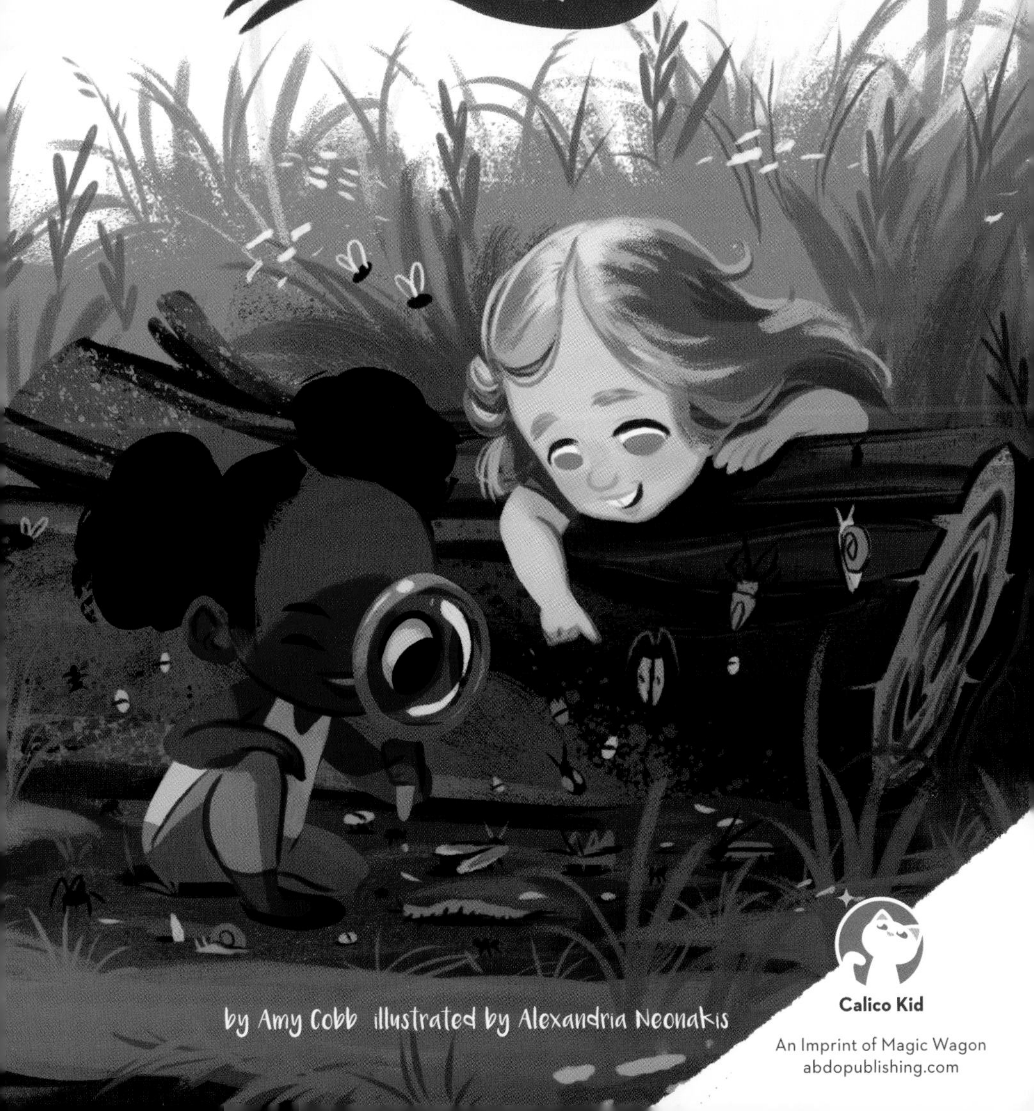

by Amy Cobb illustrated by Alexandria Neonakis

Calico Kid
An Imprint of Magic Wagon
abdopublishing.com

For Mom. Thank you for sending the dragonflies. With special appreciation to Heidi for your kindness and encouragement. –AC

For John, Gooby and Kitty, whose love and support make my career possible. –AN

abdopublishing.com

Published by Magic Wagon, a division of ABDO, PO Box 398166, Minneapolis, Minnesota 55439. Copyright © 2018 by Abdo Consulting Group, Inc. International copyrights reserved in all countries. No part of this book may be reproduced in any form without written permission from the publisher. Calico Kid™ is a trademark and logo of Magic Wagon.

Printed in the United States of America, North Mankato, Minnesota.
052017
092017

THIS BOOK CONTAINS
RECYCLED MATERIALS

Written by Amy Cobb
Illustrated by Alexandria Neonakis
Edited by Heidi M.D. Elston
Art Directed by Laura Mitchell

Publisher's Cataloging-in-Publication Data

Names: Cobb, Amy, author. | Neonakis, Alexandria, illustrator.
Title: Bug rescuer / by Amy Cobb ; illustrated by Alexandria Neonakis.
Description: Minneapolis, MN : Magic Wagon, 2018. | Series: Libby Wimbley
Summary: Libby and her friend Becca are searching for bugs to finish their nature
   worksheet for school. They come across a dragonfly trapped in an old spider
   web. Very carefully, Libby frees the dragonfly and sets it free in a new home.
Identifiers: LCCN 2017930830 | ISBN 9781532130243 (lib. bdg.) |
   ISBN 9781614798514 (ebook) | ISBN 9781614798569 (Read-to-me ebook)
Subjects: LCSH: Bugs--Juvenile fiction. | Dragonflies--Juvenile fiction. |
   Friendship--Juvenile fiction.
Classification: DDC [Fic]--dc23
LC record available at http://lccn.loc.gov/2017930830

Table of Contents

Chapter 1

The Log Roll

It was Sunday afternoon. Libby Wimbley and her best friend, Becca, planned to ride bikes.

But first, they had to look for bugs to finish their Nature Detective worksheet.

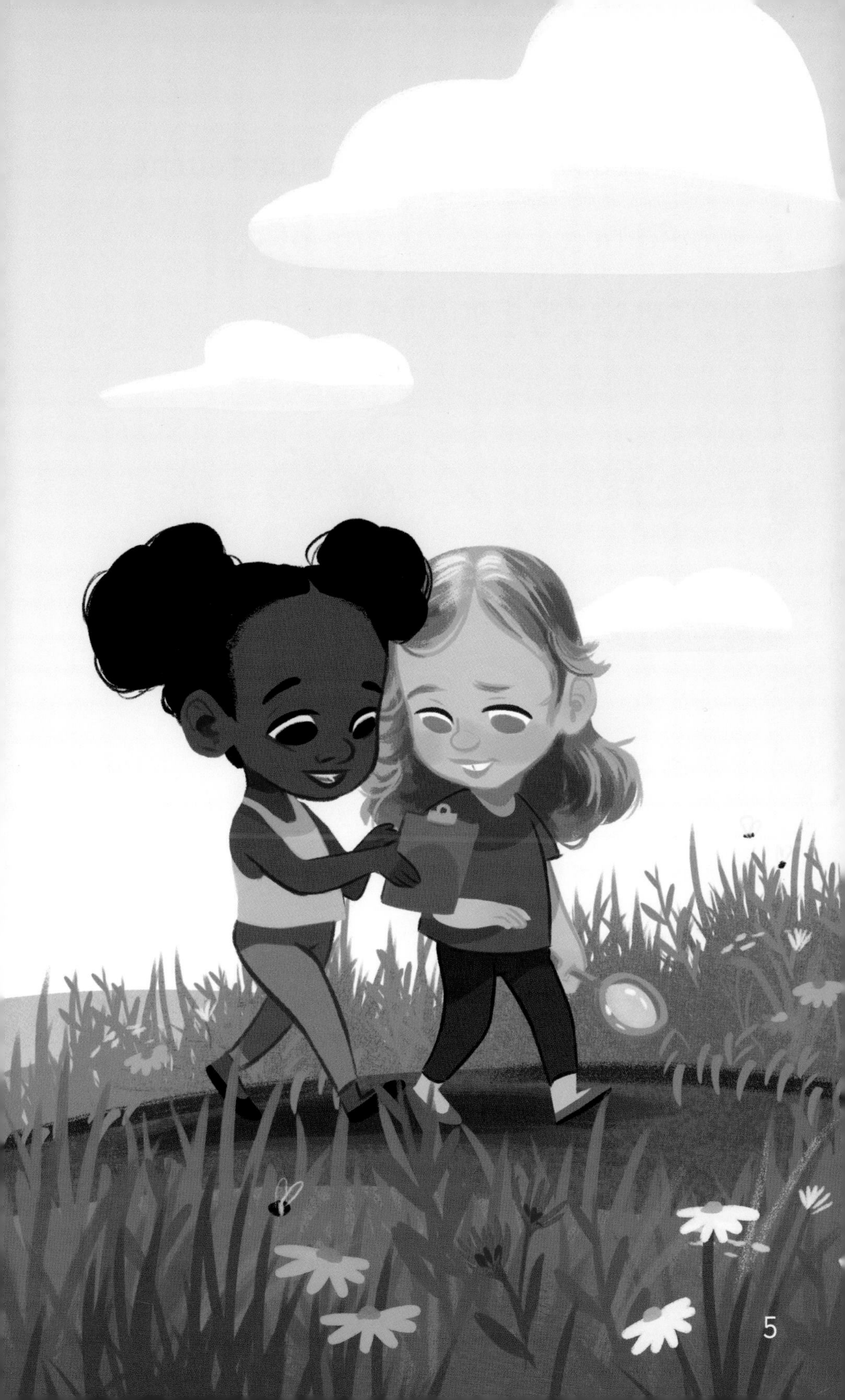

If they didn't, their science teacher would be as mad as one of the hornets they'd studied in class.

"Where should we look, Libby?" Becca asked. She stared at Libby through a magnifying glass. The lens made Becca look like a giant housefly.

“Maybe behind the barn,” Libby said. “I’ll bet bugs love the shade trees there.”

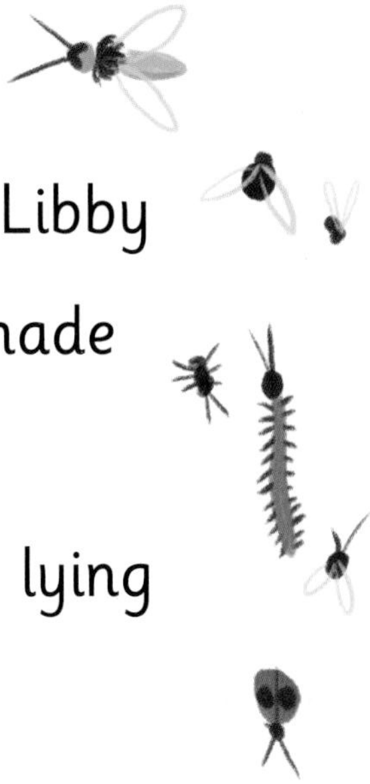

Soon, the girls found a log lying on the ground.

“Every bug on our list is probably under here,” Libby said.

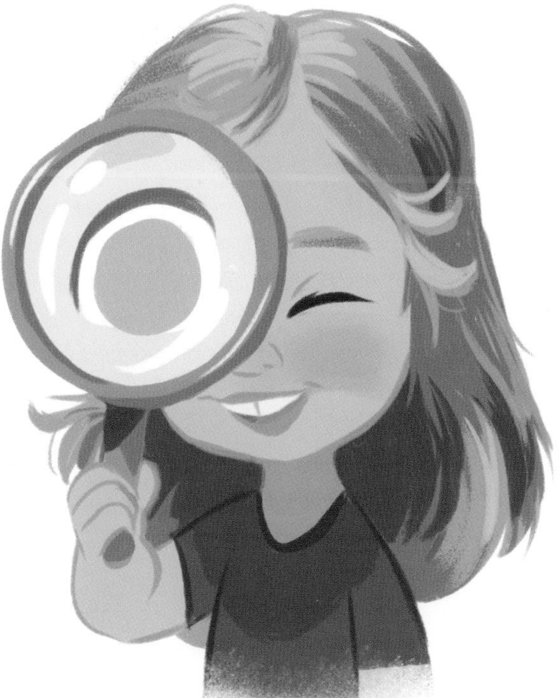

Libby and Becca rolled the log over. Damp, dark dirt lay beneath it. Tiny insects zigzagged in all directions.

"There's a balled-up roly-poly," Libby said. "Real name: pill bug."

"Check!" Becca marked it off their worksheet. "And there's a millipede!"

"Look at all of those legs!" Libby said.

Becca made another check mark. "That's all of the bugs here. Let's look somewhere else."

"Hang on!" Libby said. "First, let's roll the bugs' log home back where we found it."

"Good idea," Becca agreed.

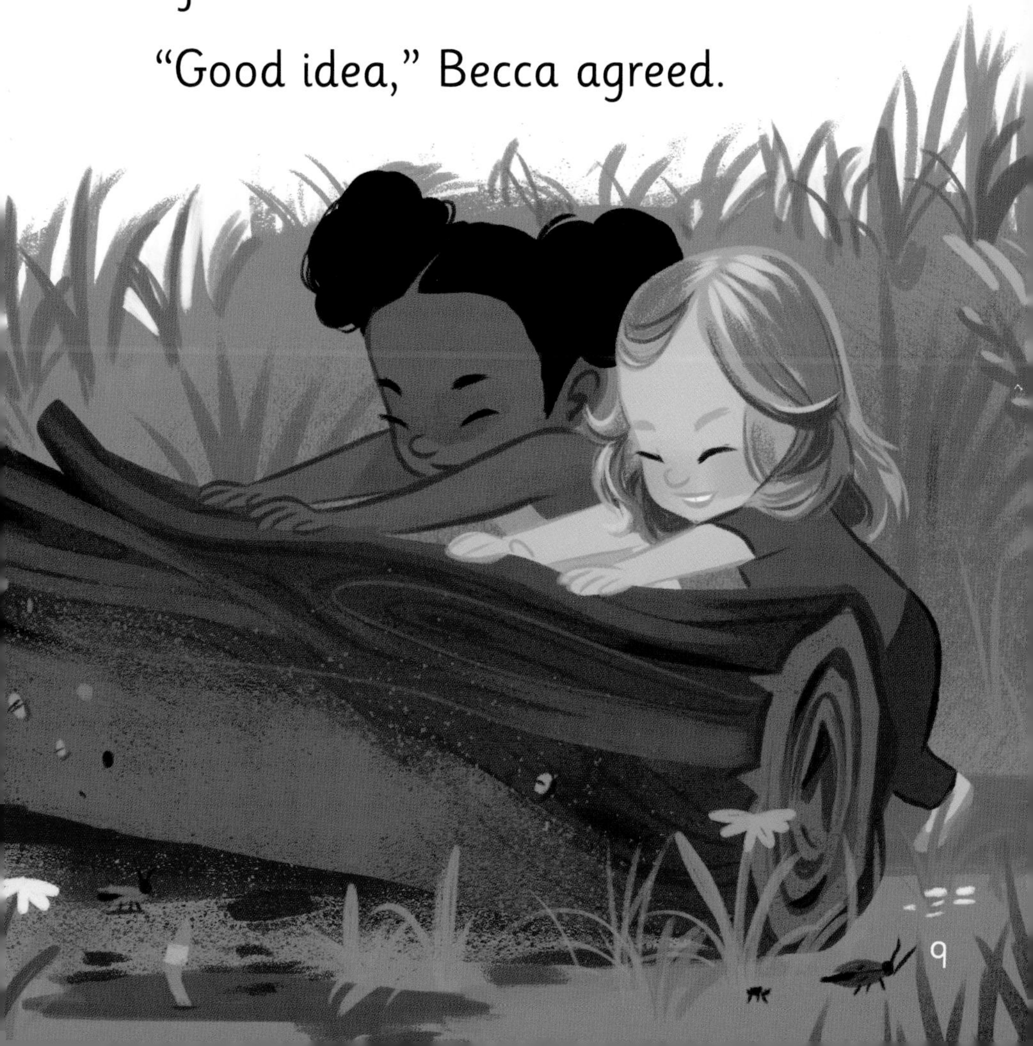

Chapter #2

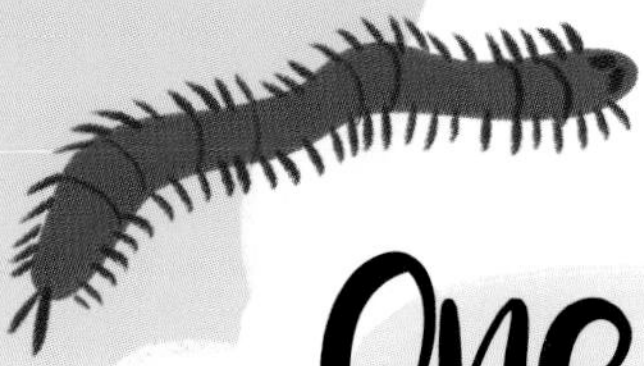

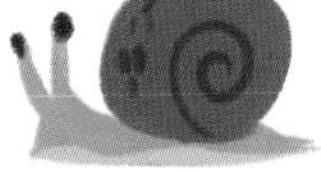

One More Bug

Once they were finished, Libby asked, "How many bugs do we have left to find?"

"Only two more," Becca said. "We're almost done."

"Yes!" Libby pumped her fists into the air. "Bikes, here we come!"

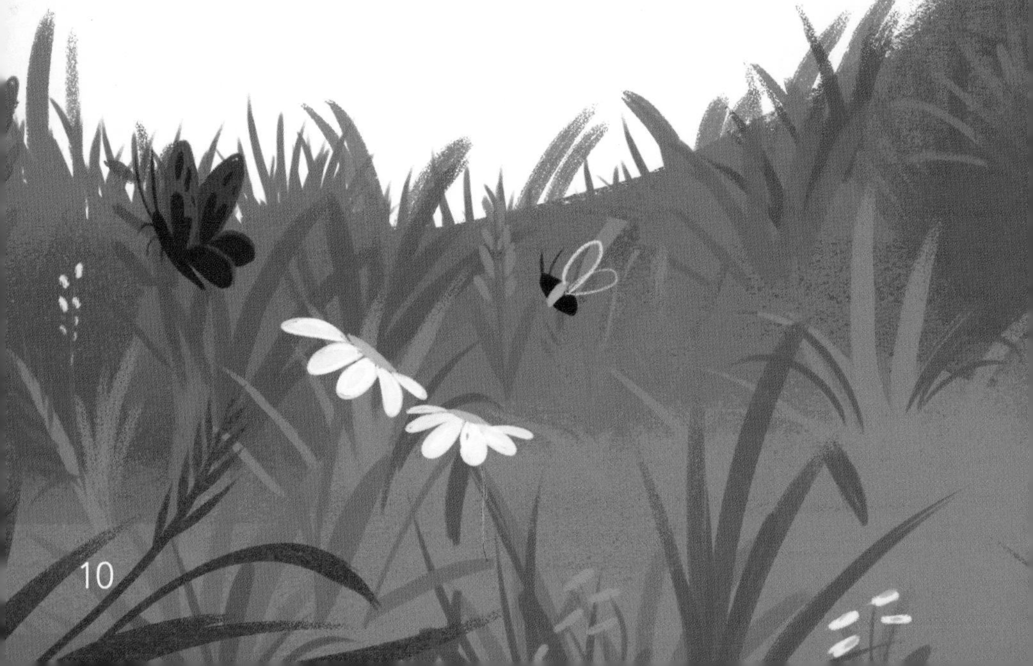

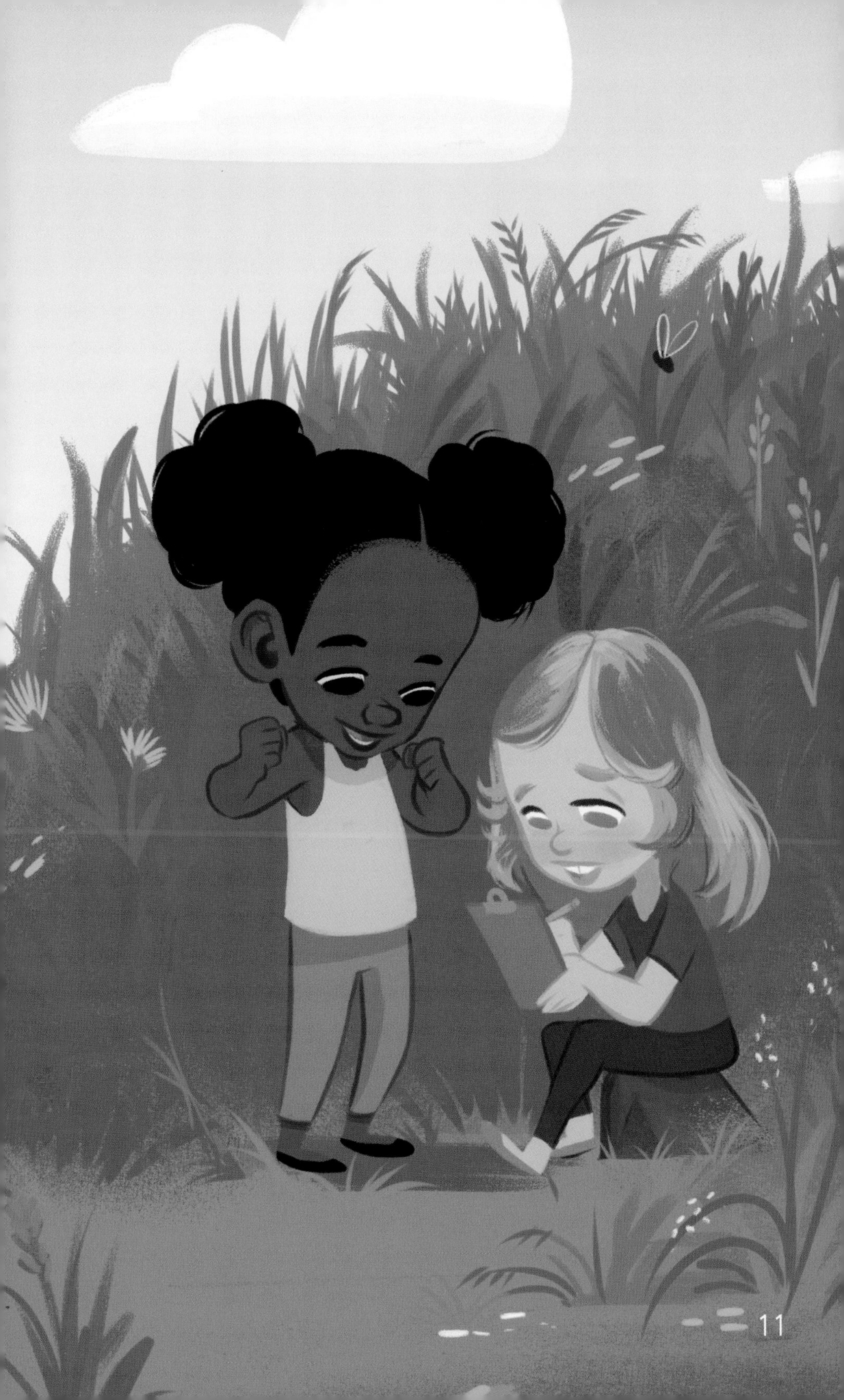

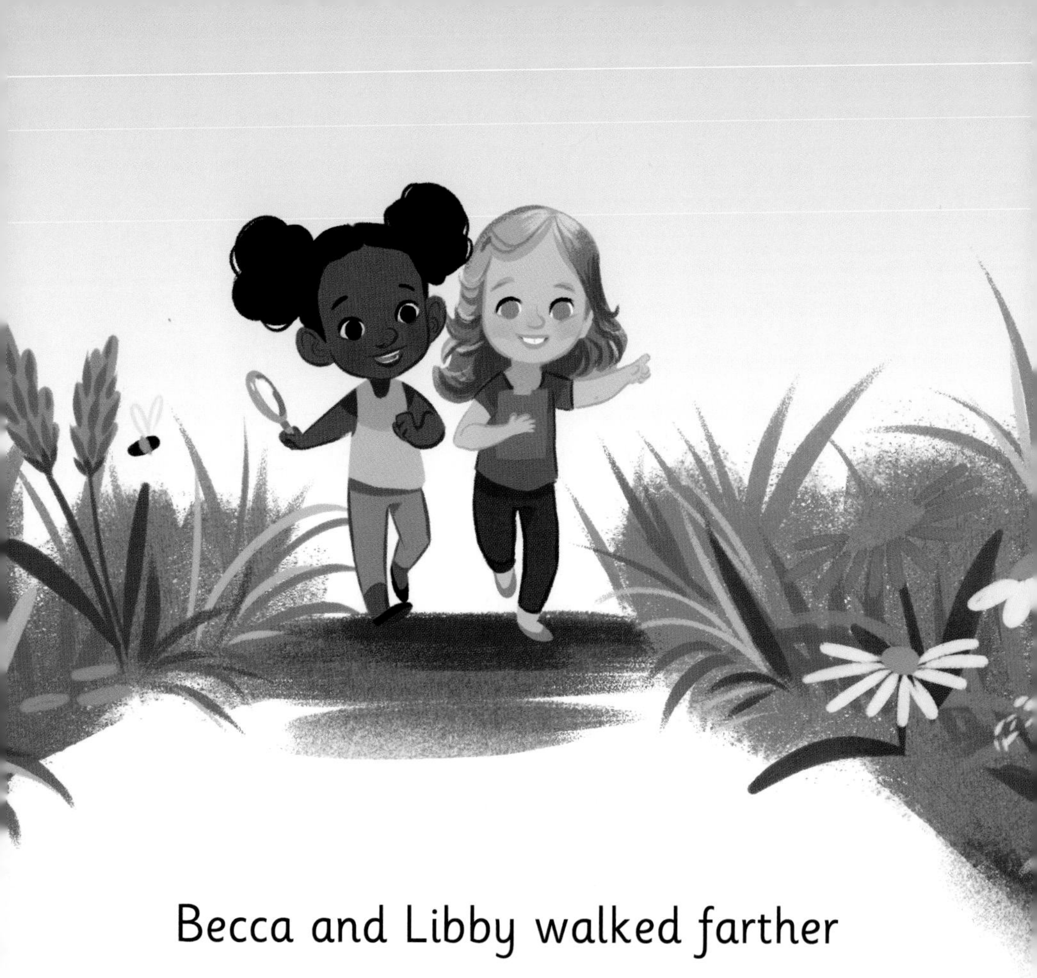

Becca and Libby walked farther along the path. Sweet-smelling wild roses grew in a thicket nearby.

"Flowers attract bugs," Libby said.

Sure enough, fuzzy yellow and black striped insects buzzed around the pink petals.

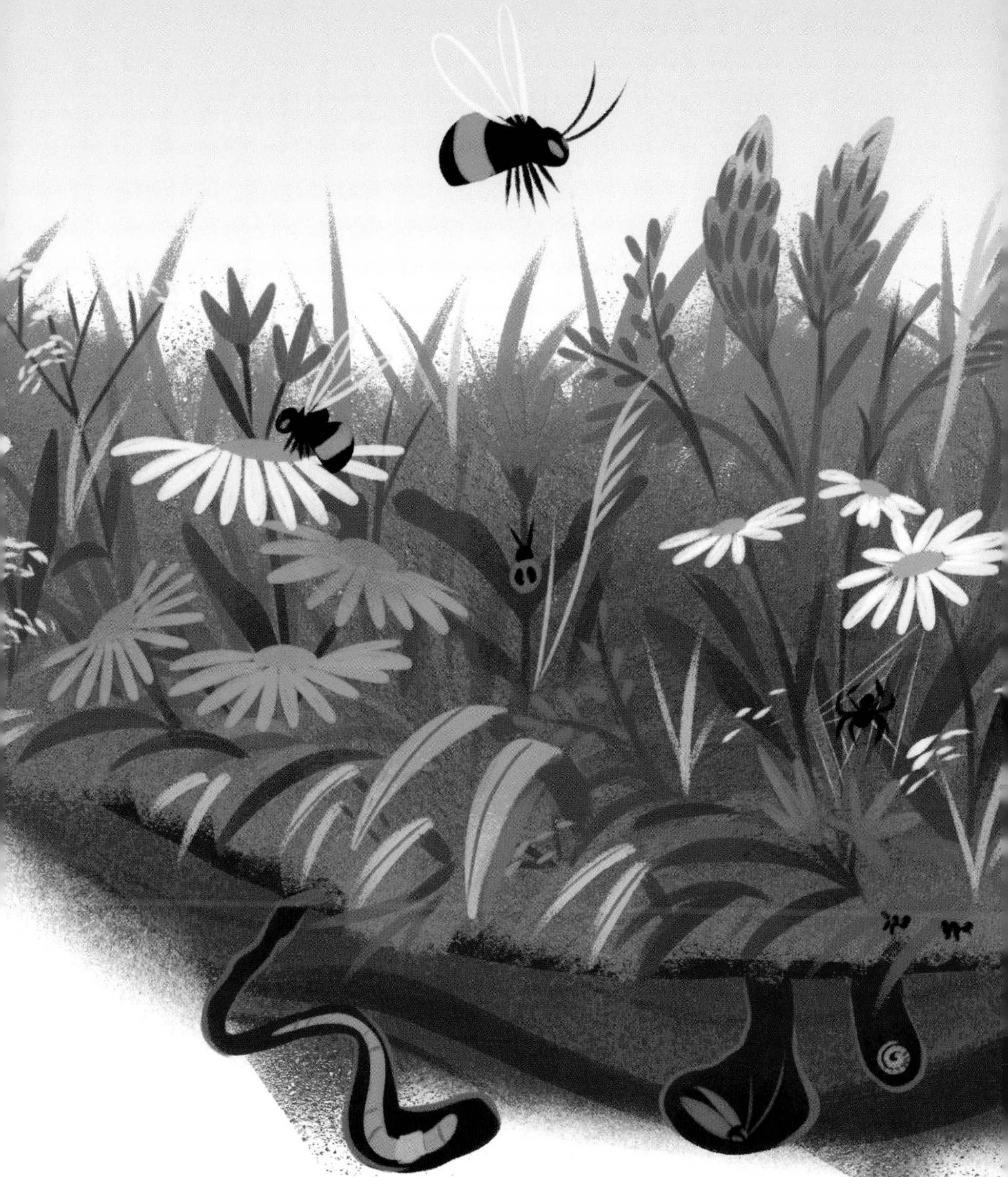

“Bees!” Becca scanned their worksheet and smiled. “Check!”

Libby looked around. “Hmm. We only have to find one more bug. Then we'll be finished.”

“How about butterflies?” Becca asked. “They're on our list.”

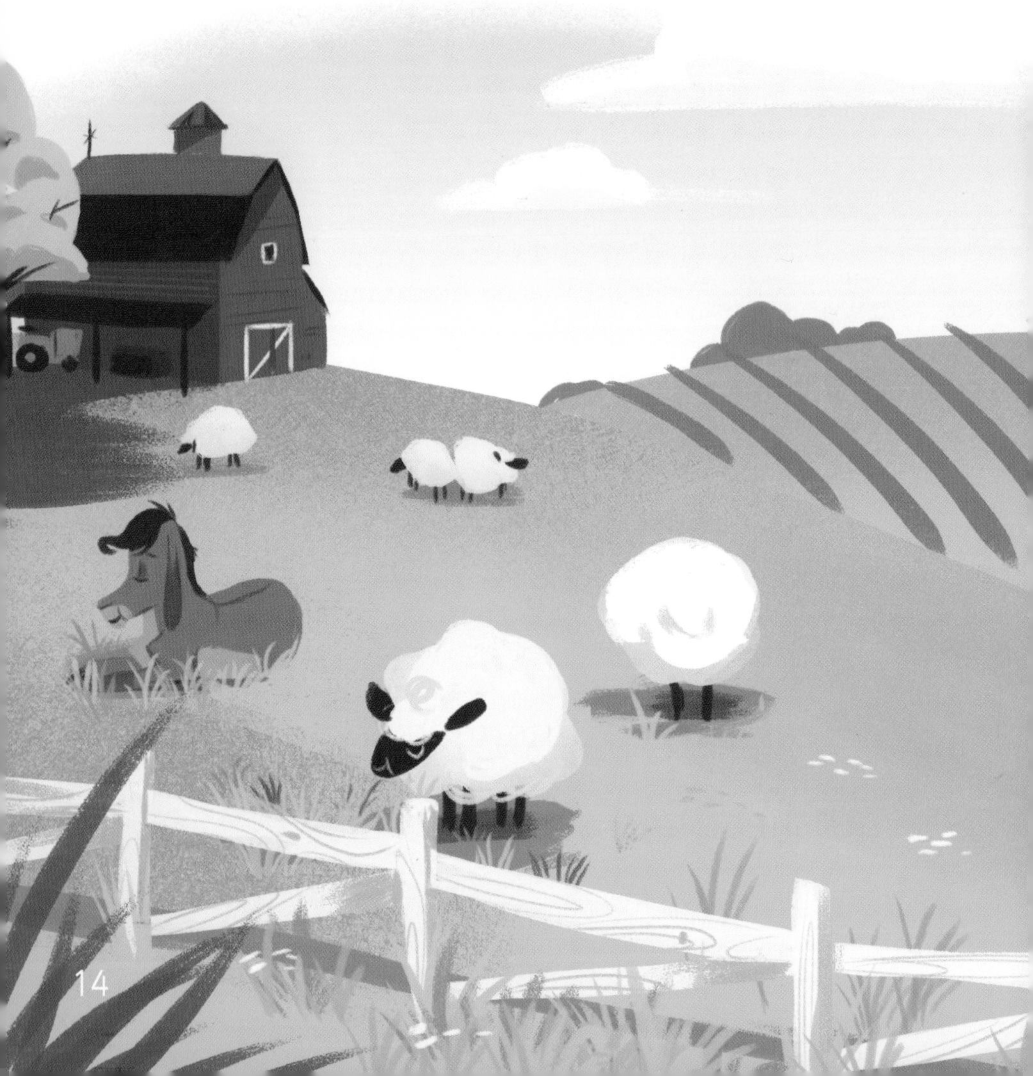

"Lucky for us, my mom planted milkweed in her flower garden. It attracts monarch butterflies," Libby said.

"I'll race you there!" Becca said, zooming back toward the house.

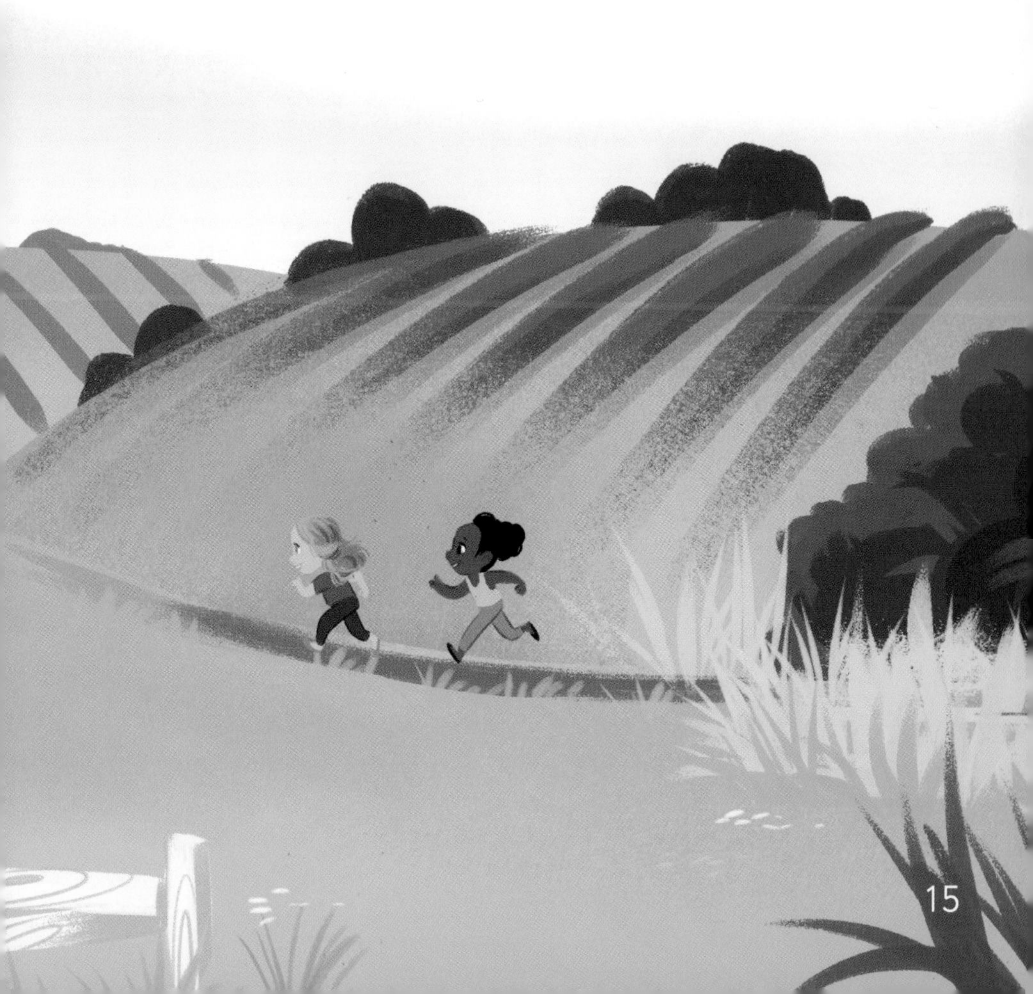

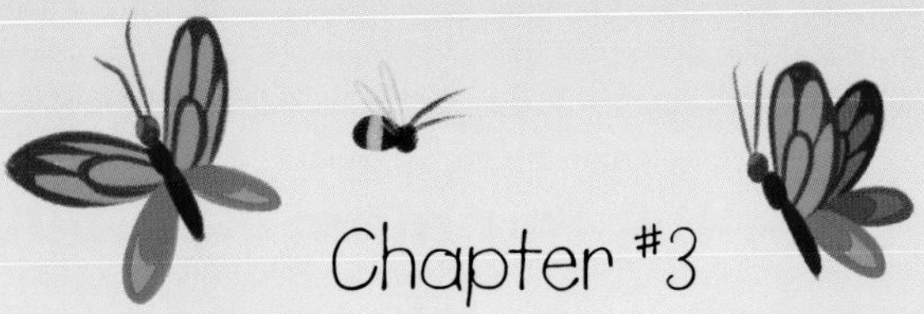

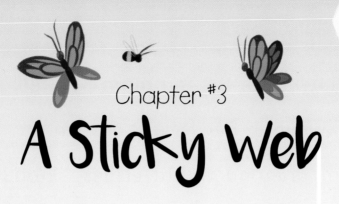

Chapter #3

A Sticky Web

Becca was a fast runner. She ran ahead and waited for Libby on the log they'd rolled over earlier.

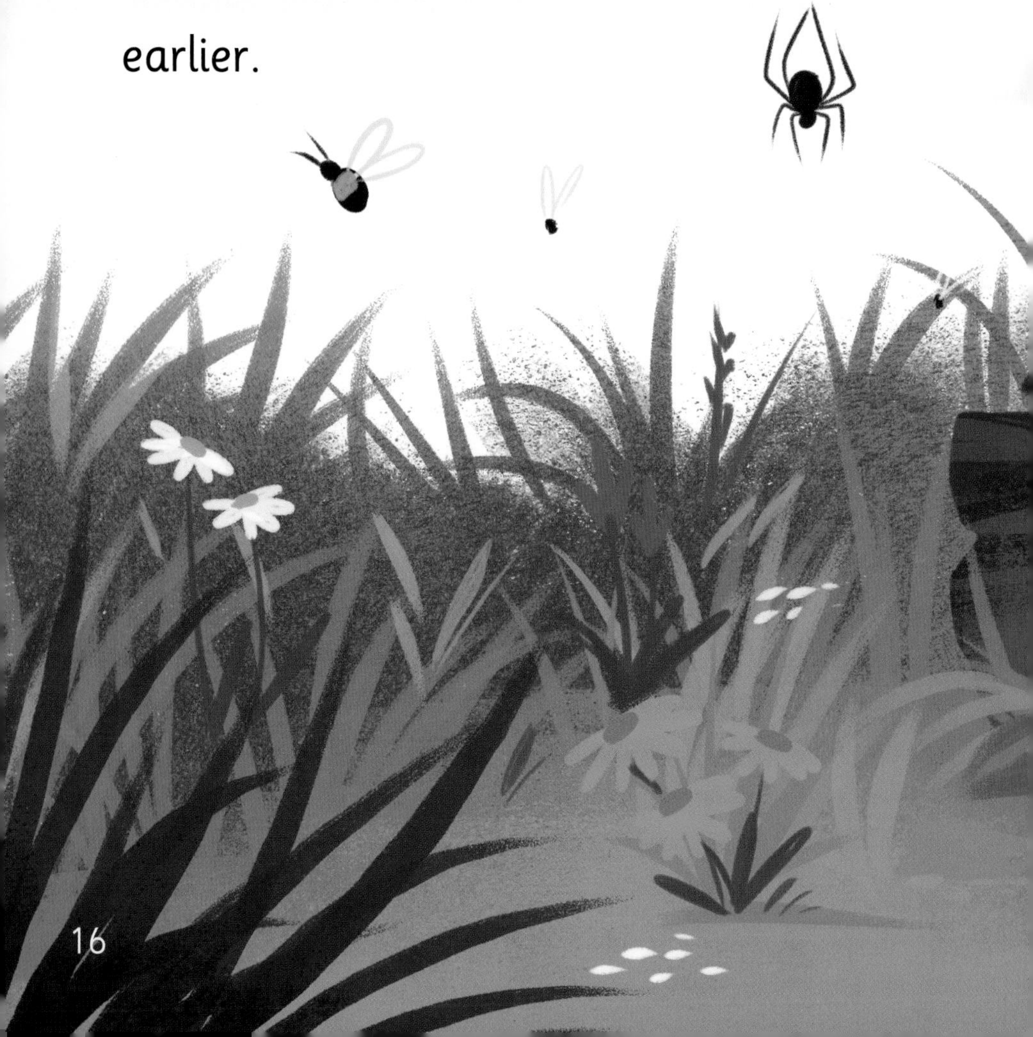

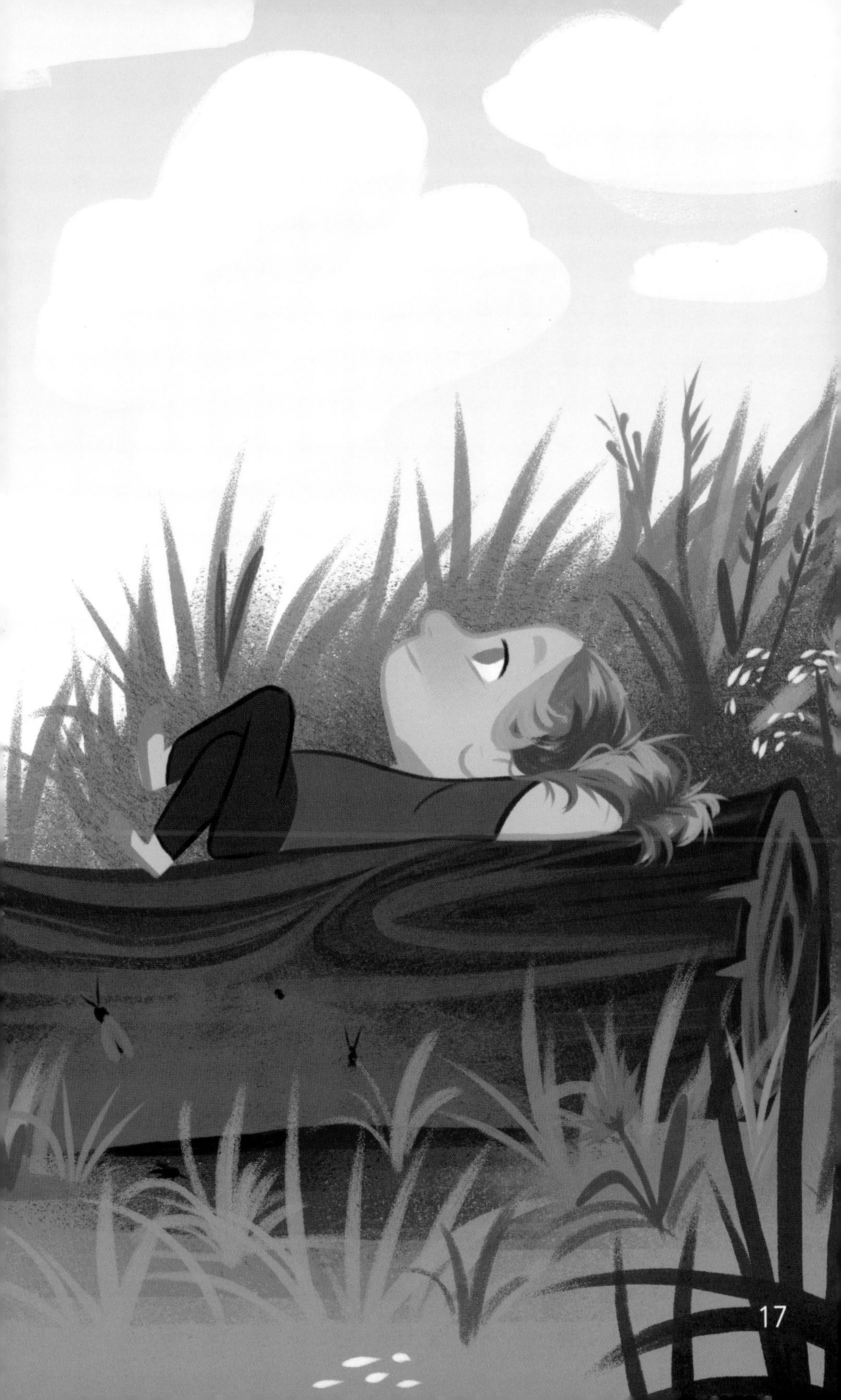

Libby sat beside Becca. "Are mosquitoes on our list? I hear one buzzing around."

Becca leaned over to swat it away. "Uh, oh," she said, looking past Libby.

"What?" Libby turned to look, too.

"You're sitting next to—" Becca began.

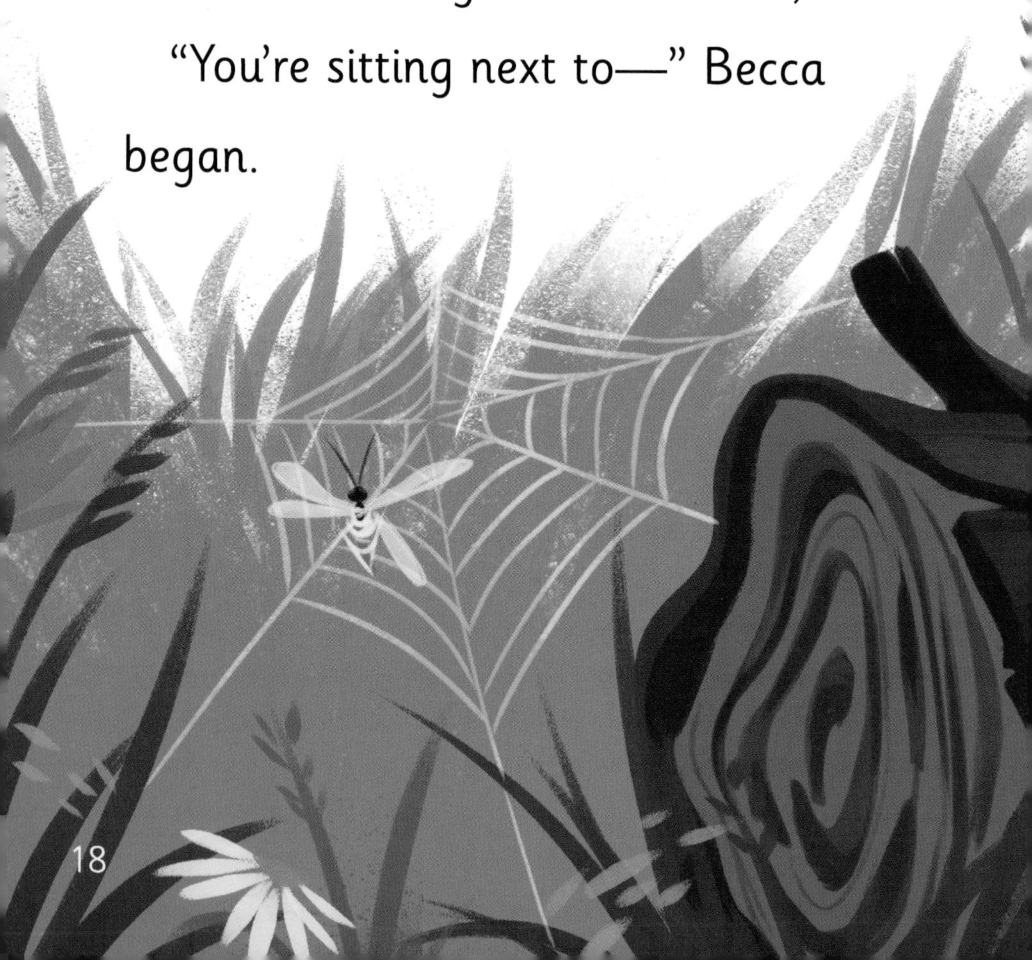

"A spider web!" the girls screamed at the same time.

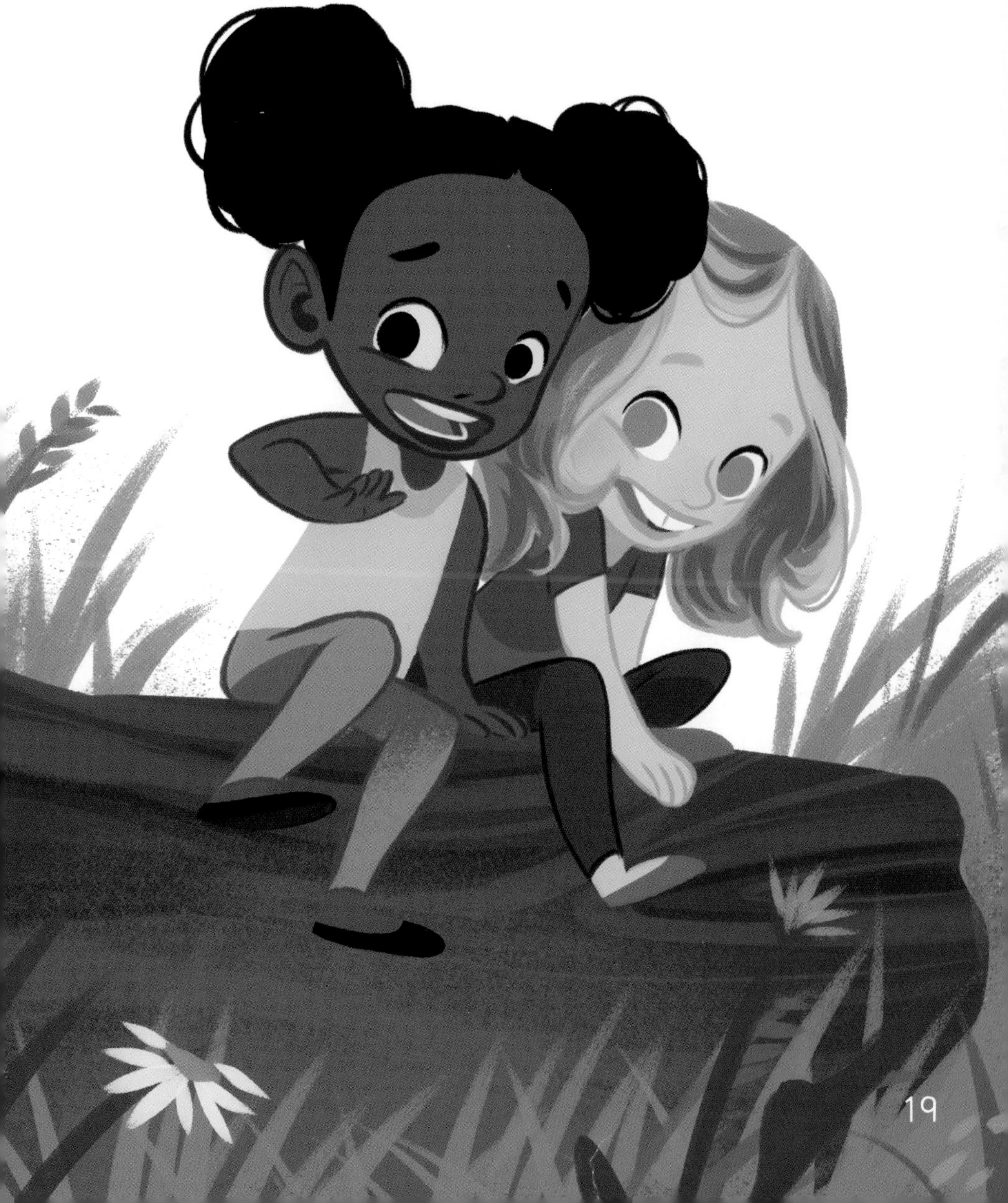

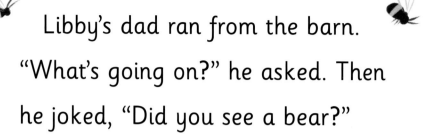

Libby's dad ran from the barn. "What's going on?" he asked. Then he joked, "Did you see a bear?"

"No bears here, Dad!" Libby laughed.

Becca laughed, too. "And no spiders either," she said. "This is an old web. The spider doesn't live here anymore."

“But look!” Libby pointed to the sticky strands.

The web was moving. It wasn’t the spider’s home now, but a bug was stuck.

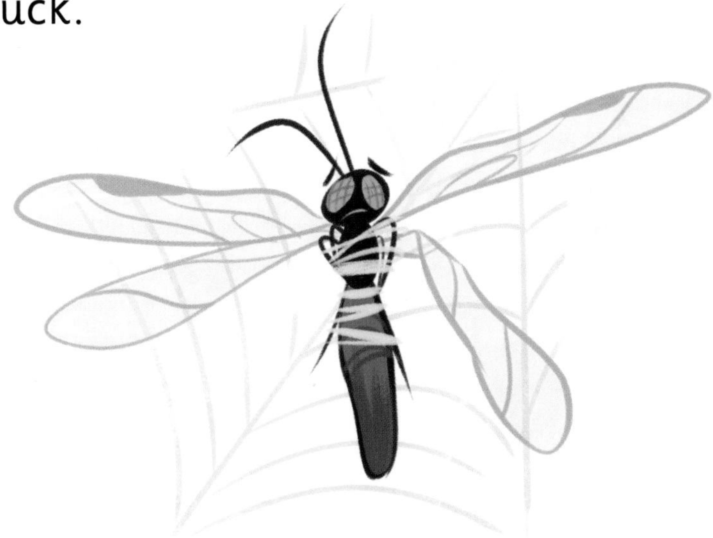

“What is it?” Becca asked.

Libby took a closer look. “It’s a dragonfly,” she said. “We have to set it free!”

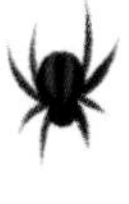

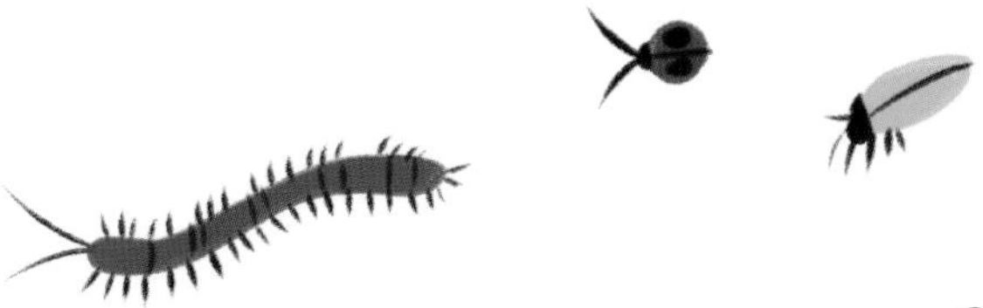

Chapter #4

Set Free

Dad shook his head. "I don't think we can help the dragonfly, Libby."

"But we have to try," Libby said.

"Please, Mr. Wimbley," Becca said.

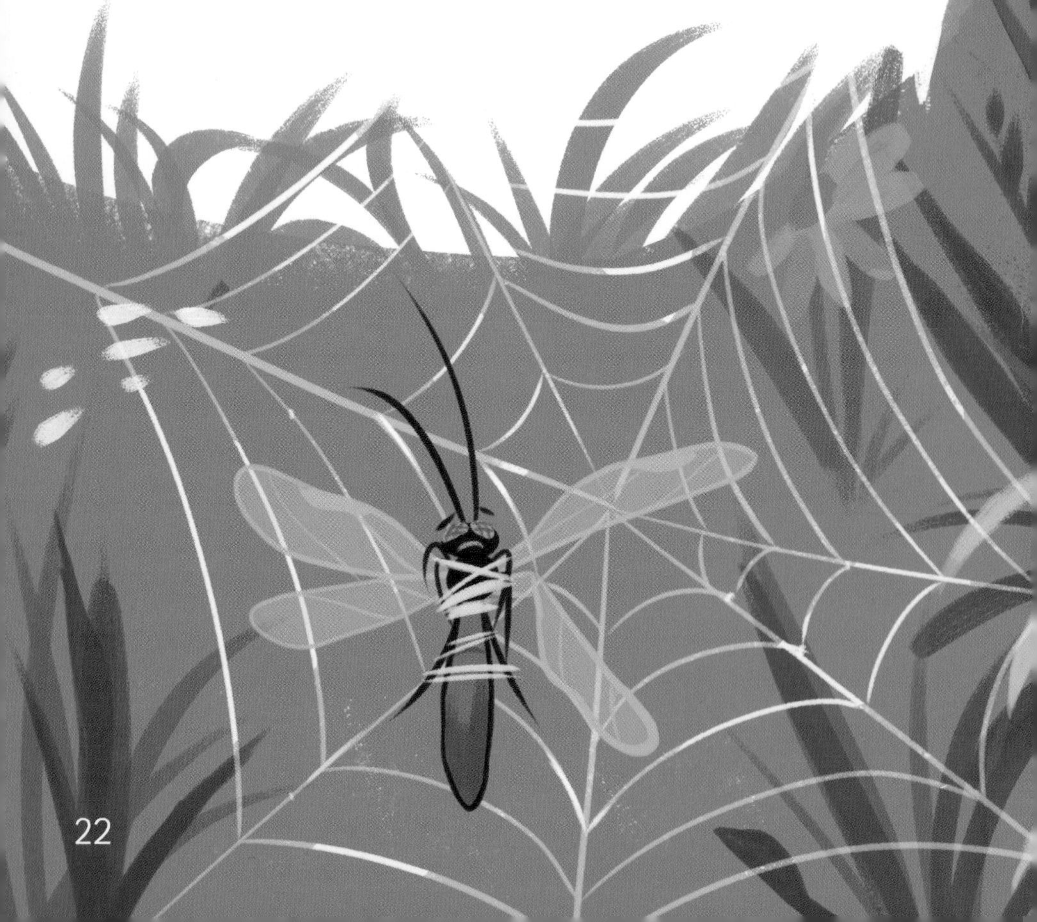

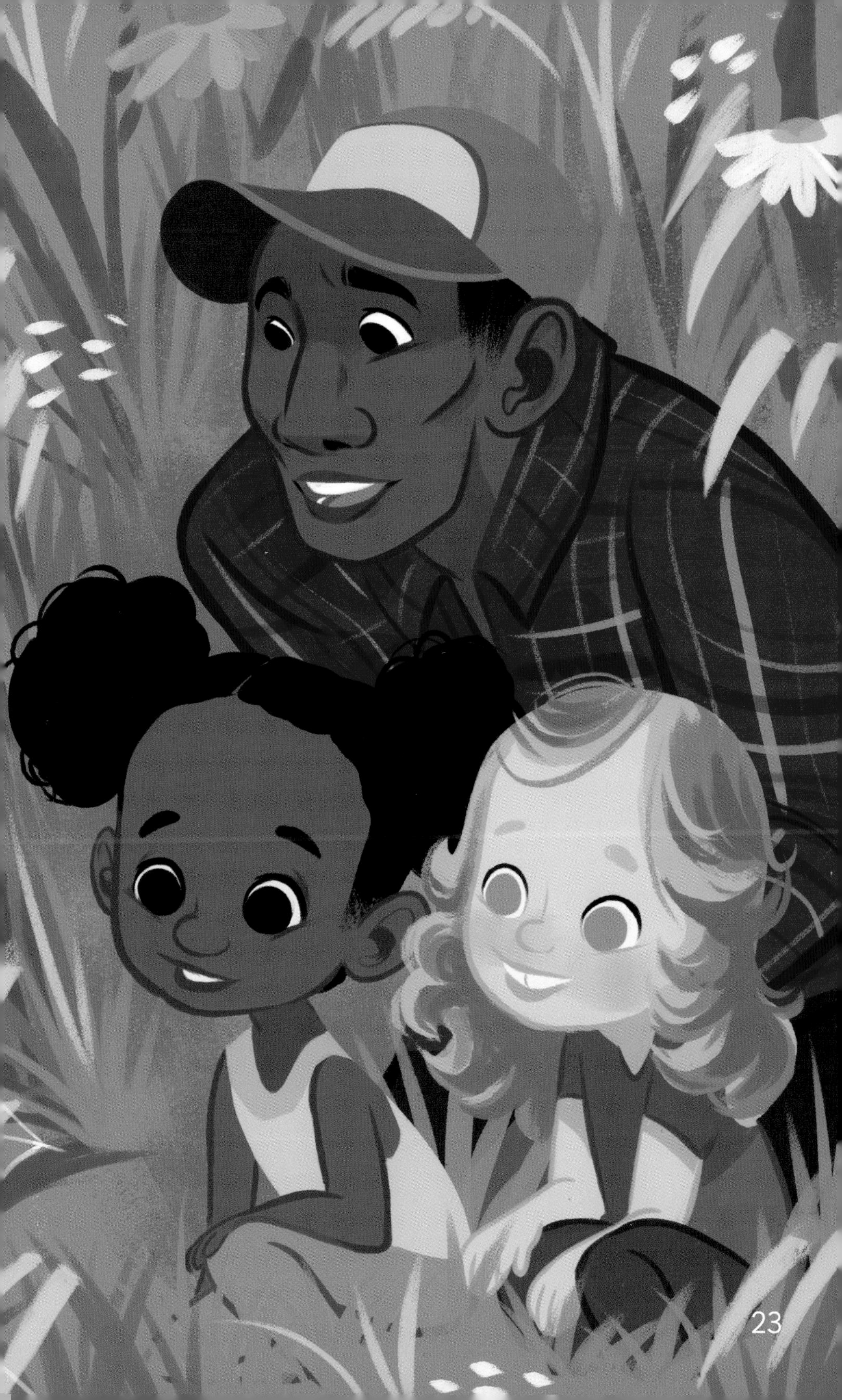

Dad handed Libby a pair of gloves.
"Here," he said. "Put these on first.
But remember, this may not work."

"Okay," Libby said, sliding her
hands into the gloves.

Dad and Becca held the web still
while Libby set to work.

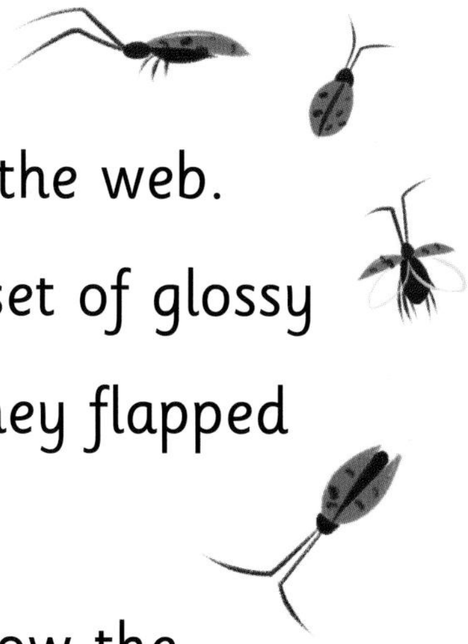

Libby gently pulled on the web.
First, she untangled one set of glossy
wings. Then the other. They flapped
up and down.

"There," Libby said. "Now the
dragonfly can move its wings."

Becca nodded. "But you still have to release its legs."

"Be careful," Dad said.

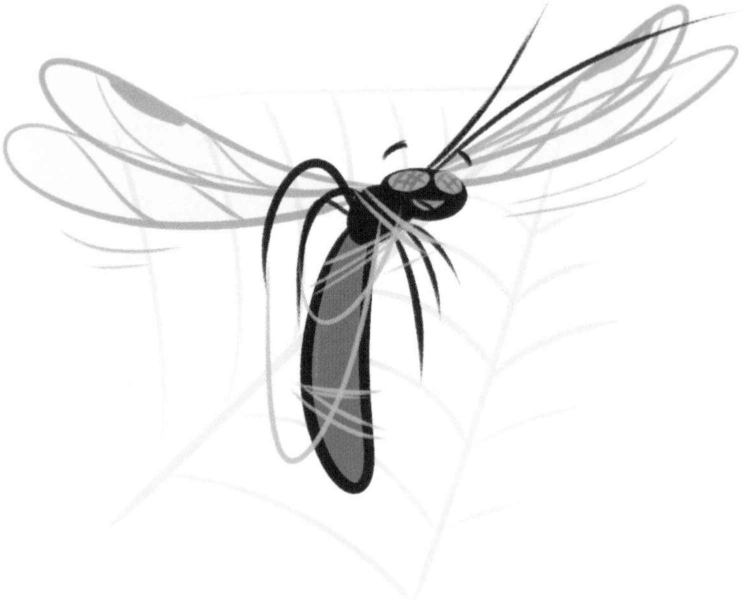

Untangling the legs wasn't easy. There were six of them. And they were tiny.

Libby was gentle. She was very careful, too, just like Dad said.

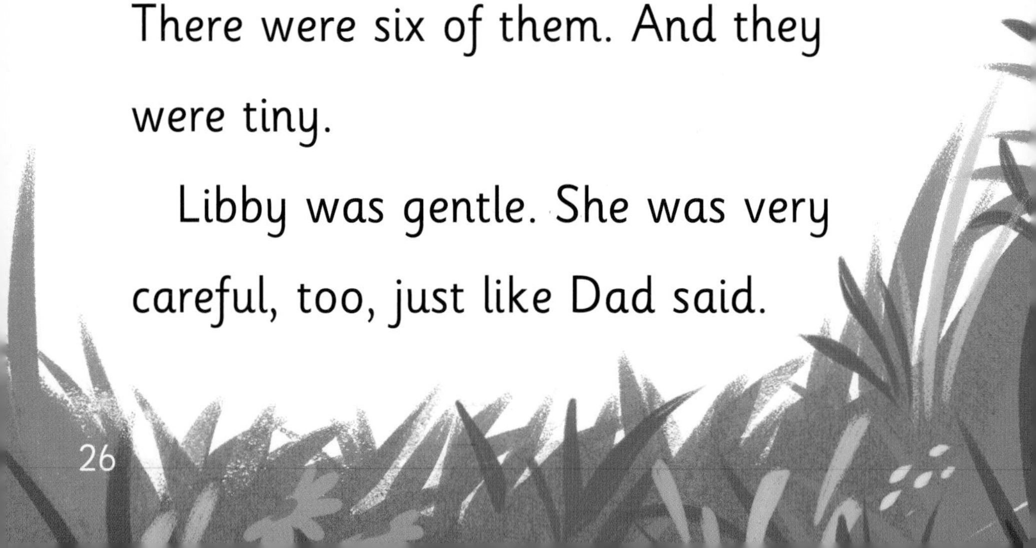

Before long, the dragonfly wasn't trapped in the spider web anymore. Now it was free.

"Yay, Libby!" Becca smiled.

So did Dad.

And Libby smiled too. The dragonfly was cupped safely inside her hands.

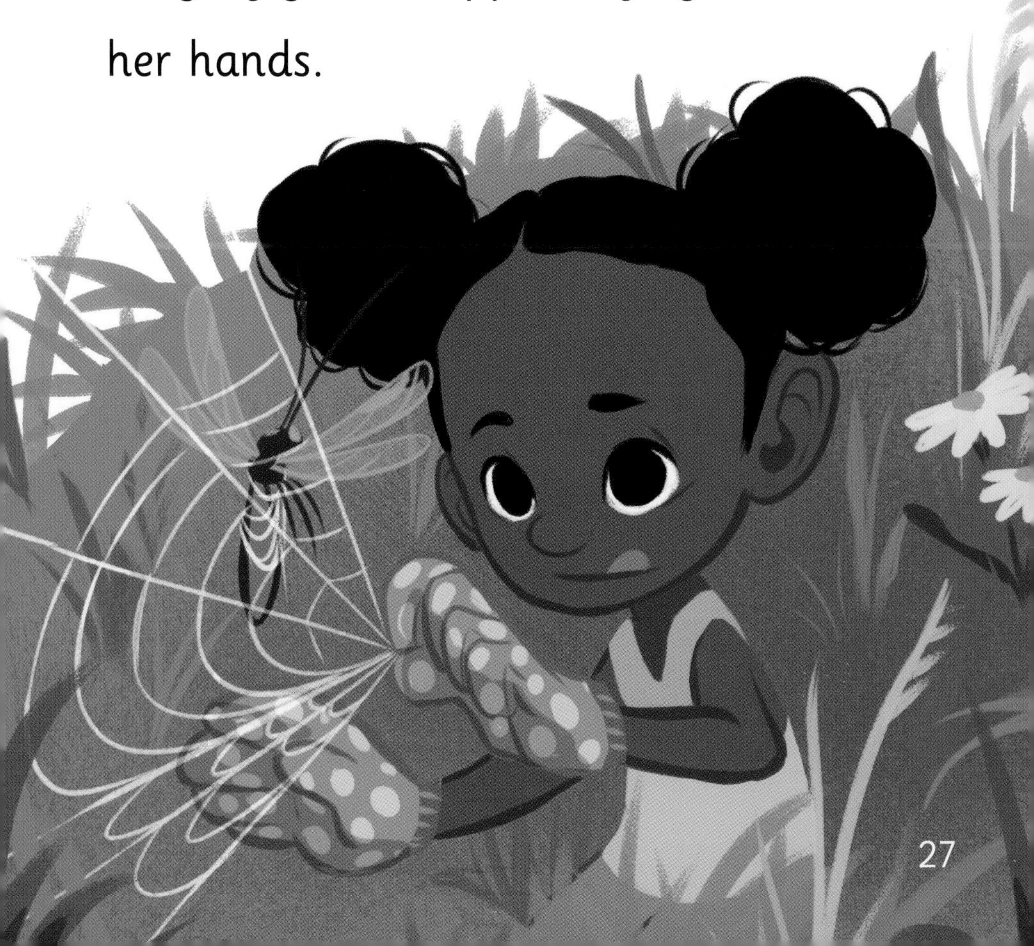

Chapter 5

A New Home

Becca frowned. "Libby, why aren't you letting the dragonfly go?"

"I will," Libby said. "But not here. This isn't a good dragonfly home."

"It isn't?" Becca asked.

Libby shook her head. "Dragonflies like water. And plants to rest on. And a place to catch bugs for food," she said.

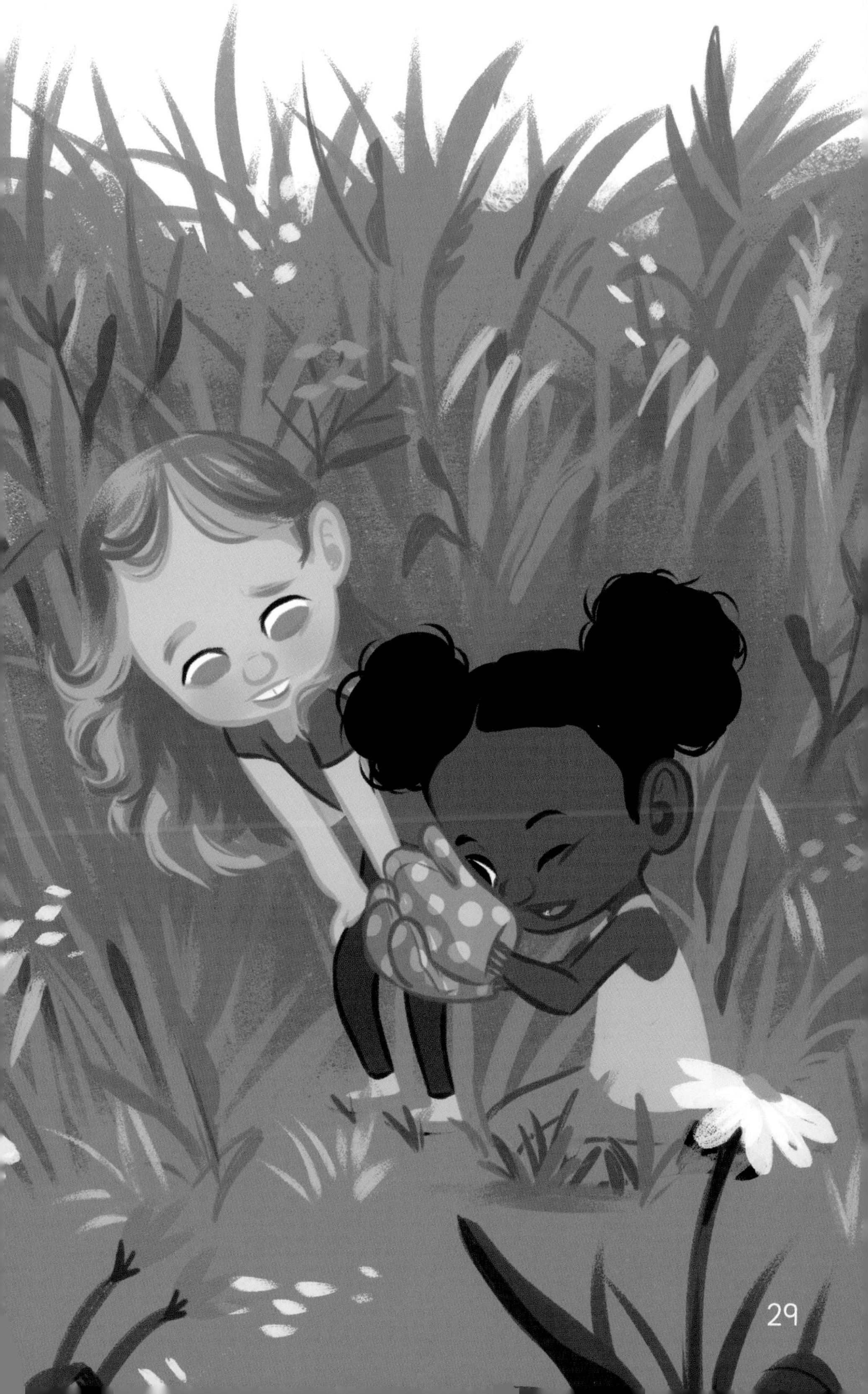

Then Libby thought for a second.
"I know the perfect spot. Follow me!"
They took the path down to the
pond.

Other dragonflies flitted above the
still green water. Cattails and tall,
thin reeds grew around the edge.
Other bugs lived at the pond, too.

"Welcome to your new home,"
Libby said. She opened her hands.
The dragonfly flapped its wings. Then
it flew away.

Becca said, "I think it likes it here."

"Me, too." Libby smiled.

Libby and Becca checked the last
bug—a dragonfly—off their science
worksheet.

"You know, being a nature detective is fun," Libby said. "But there's something even better."

Becca looked surprised. "What's that?"

"Being a bug rescuer!" Libby laughed. "Let's see if more bugs need our help."

Libby and Becca pedaled off into the afternoon sunshine.